Scrappers

#9
GRAND SLAM

Dean Hughes

ALADDIN PAPERBACKS

First Aladdin Paperbacks edition October 1999

Copyright © 1999 by Dean Hughes

Aladdin Paperbacks
An imprint of Simon & Schuster
Children's Publishing Division
1230 Avenue of the Americas
New York, NY 10020

Also available in an Atheneum Books for Young Readers hardcover edition.

The text for this book was set in Caslon 540 Roman.

Printed and bound in the United States of America

10   9   8   7   6   5   4   3   2   1

The Library of Congress has cataloged the hardcover edition as follows:
Hughes, Dean, 1943–
Grand slam / by Dean Hughes.
p.   cm.—(Scrappers ; #9)
Summary: Just as Thurlow feels that he may be able to lead the Scrappers singlehandedly to the season championship, an injury sidelines him and threatens to take away their victory.
ISBN 0-689-81932-3 (hardcover).—ISBN 0-689-81942-0 (pbk.)
[1. Baseball—Fiction.] I. Title.
II. Series: Hughes, Dean, 1943-   Scrappers; #9.
PZ7.H87312Gr   1999   [Fic]—dc21   99-20417

CHAPTER ONE

Thurlow Coates was late arriving for the game against the Mustangs. He waited at home and then walked to the park, even though his mother had gone ahead in the car. The truth was, he liked to arrive at the last minute. He didn't like to spend a lot of time out in the heat before the game started.

As soon as Thurlow sat down on the grass to put on his cleats, Coach Carlton started in on one of his speeches. The coach was a good guy, and Thurlow had gotten to like him, but the man gave a few too many pep talks.

"Okay, kids, this is it. This is what we've been playing for all summer. If we beat the Mustangs today, we win the second-half championship. And if we do that, we get to play them again next week—under the lights over at the college. That one would be for all the marbles."

Thurlow put a double knot in his shoelaces, then glanced around at the other players. He couldn't believe how nervous they seemed. Jeremy Lim looked worried enough to puke. And Gloria Gibbs was trying to look *bad*. How she really looked was uptight and jittery.

"Let's use what we've been learning," Coach Carlton said. "Let's play with confidence and with some *fire*—but let's also have a great time. This is fun."

Thurlow wasn't worried. He knew he would come through. He always played his best in big games.

"Okay, it's our turn to take the field for some infield. Let's go."

Thurlow got up slowly. He hadn't stretched, so he did a couple of toe touches and bent sideways at the waist a few times. Then he grabbed his glove and jogged toward the field. As he passed third base, Robbie Marquez said, "Man, this is the big one. We've gotta have it."

"We'll get 'em," Thurlow told him.

"I guess. I just hope I don't mess up."

"Naw. You'll be all right," Thurlow said. "I plan to do some *damage* today. You can depend on that."

"All right!"

Thurlow did want to beat the Mustangs—and beat them bad. But what he liked even more was being the player everyone *knew* would get the job done.

Adam Pfitzer was pitching for the Scrappers today. He seemed really pumped up. During warm-up he was steaming the ball. But when the leadoff batter stepped in and the game was finally under way, Adam let fly with a pitch that was way over the head of his catcher, Wilson Love. The ball slammed against the screen, halfway up the backstop. Maybe Adam was a little *too* pumped up.

Thurlow winced a little in the outfield. He could only do so much. If Adam couldn't throw strikes, there was no way the Scrappers were going to beat the Mustangs.

The next pitch was just as hard and still a little high, but Billy Mauer, the Mustangs' leadoff hitter, was eager too. He took a big cut and missed.

Adam never did get a pitch in the strike zone, but Mauer went down swinging anyway, and Mr. London, the Mustangs' coach, got all over him.

But the strikeout seemed to relax Adam. He took a big breath and then peppered a fastball over the plate. Eddie Donaldson swung hard and lifted a high fly toward Jeremy in right field.

Jeremy dashed forward before he had time to get a bead on the ball. Then he stopped just as suddenly as he had started. Quickly, he dropped back a few steps, reached up, and stabbed the ball with one hand.

Two outs.

But Thurlow was taking a deep breath himself now.

"I'm too psyched up," Jeremy yelled to Thurlow. "I haven't made that mistake in a long time."

Earlier in the season Jeremy had had a tendency to take off after a ball before he really had a chance to judge where it was going. What was he doing now? Forgetting everything he had learned?

Thurlow *was* going to have to do something today.

"Hey, Lim, where you going?" Donaldson yelled. "Yo' mama call you?"

The Mustangs weren't usually hot dogs, but they were strung pretty tight themselves today. They had to be thinking that they didn't want to blow this game and end up having to play again.

All summer they had led the league, but the Scrappers had beaten them once before—and that had to give them something to think about.

Sheri Gibby was up. She let a couple go by and then got a good fastball and *whacked* it to left center. The ball was heading for the fence, but Thurlow didn't give up on it. He ran all out, and the ball seemed to float a little more than he had thought it might.

Still, it was going to be over his head. . . .

And then he leaped—really got up—stretched his arm high, and felt the ball hit the pocket of his glove.

And stick.

He had actually surprised himself. But he didn't let anyone see that. He took his time turning back to the infield, and then he tossed the ball to Trent Lubak, who had also been chasing it—at half the speed.

"There's *no way!*" Trent said, his voice full of amazement. "You *couldn't* have caught that ball."

"I didn't. I had one in my pocket," Thurlow joked. "It was all a trick."

Then, as he trotted toward the infield, he acted as though he couldn't hear all the cheering. He headed to the dugout and, without saying a word, took a seat on the bench.

What he hoped was that the Scrappers would get into the game now, maybe calm down a little. But Jeremy walked to the plate, looking way too stiff. He stood like a statue as he watched Justin Lou take his last warm-up pitch.

Thurlow wondered why Lou was on the mound. Derek Salinas was the Mustangs' best pitcher. Maybe Salinas's arm was tired. He had pitched a few days before. Or maybe Mr. London was thinking that if the season did come down to one more game, he wanted Salinas on the mound then.

Jeremy still looked like a statue when he stepped into the box. He hadn't stood up this straight in the box all season. Lou threw a pitch outside, and Jeremy didn't move. The kid was looking for a walk, all the way.

Lou had to have seen that, too. But he was probably a little too pumped himself. He tried to bust Jeremy in tight and got the ball too close. Jeremy didn't react until the last second. As he spun away, the ball glanced off his shoulder.

"Take your base!" the ump shouted.

The Scrappers all jumped up as though Jeremy had just hammered one over the fence.

"All right! We got it going now!" they were yelling.

Thurlow kept his seat.

Coach Carlton shouted, "Robbie, take it easy. Just stand in there and take a good swing. We can hit Lou."

Robbie nodded . . . and then walked to the plate and forgot everything the coach had said. He took a woodchopper cut at a high pitch and missed. Then he let a fat one, down the middle, go by.

He stepped out and slammed his bat against the ground. But when he stepped back in, he swung at a high fastball and sent a pop-up straight in the air.

Big Brandon Flowers, the Mustangs' catcher, stood his ground, finally moved forward a step, and made the catch.

One away. A ball on the infield, to the right side, would have moved Jeremy to second and, with Jeremy's speed, put him in a strong position to score. Thurlow couldn't believe that Robbie, of all people, would start swinging at bad pitches.

But Thurlow was glad that the coach had shaken up the lineup a bit for today's game, because he'd be at bat sooner than usual. Wilson was up next, so Thurlow strolled over to the on-deck circle.

He found his favorite bat. It wasn't heavy, considering how big and strong Thurlow was. He liked a bat he could get around quickly—really lash.

Wilson was stepping to the plate now. Thurlow hoped the big guy would get on base somehow. Thurlow wanted to unload on one— the more runners on base the better.

But Wilson must have been watching Robbie. He got a high pitch and took a blind cut at it. And he popped the ball up, too. This one drifted toward Alan Pingree, the first baseman. Pingree shaded his eyes from the sun, trotted toward the mound, and hauled it in.

Two out, and now it was up to Thurlow.

As he walked to the plate, the Scrappers were whooping it up. "Look out, Mustangs," Chad Corrigan yelled. "Thurlow's going yard on you guys."

Wanda Coates, the first base coach—and Thurlow's mother—was clapping her hands. "Come on, son. Just meet the ball," she yelled. Mrs. Coates was a big woman, tall and red-haired.

She could make enough noise to be heard over any crowd.

But Thurlow didn't like that—especially his mom calling him "son" in front of everyone. He and his mother had battled this summer after she pressured him to play on this team. The two of them had ironed some things out lately, but that still didn't mean that he liked having his mother out there on the field with him.

What Thurlow did like was the noise coming from the Mustangs. They were shouting, "Thurlow can't hit you, Justin. Don't worry about him."

But that's not what they were really thinking, and Thurlow knew it. They knew Thurlow was the *man*, the guy they had to get out—or pitch around—if they were going to beat the Scrappers.

Lou's first pitch was up high, like so many he had already thrown today. The guy was trying to finish off the season, blow the Scrappers away, but he was forcing the ball too much, and it was getting away from him.

Thurlow didn't care. What he liked was that Lou wasn't tossing outside pitches, trying to get Thurlow to nibble at something off the plate.

He was coming after him, and that's just what Thurlow wanted.

The next pitch was even with Thurlow's shoulders, and it was all he could do to lay off. But now he was ahead in the count, 2 and 0, and in good shape.

He adjusted his helmet and then got set— coiled, ready. Early in the season, he hadn't cared one way or the other what happened to the Scrappers; he had stood at the plate like a guy hanging out on a corner. Now he was serious, and he wanted the Mustangs to know it.

Lou let another one fly—a burner—and this time it was in the strike zone. Thurlow's bat jumped to the ball, met it clean, and the ball took off like a launched rocket.

Thurlow dropped his bat, turned toward left field, and watched. It was a monster shot over the fence. He lost sight of it as it dropped beyond some trees, halfway across the park.

By then he had begun his trot. He didn't show off. He simply jogged around the bases. He looked at no one, didn't acknowledge the wild cheers from his bench or from the crowd.

He did smile just a little when he saw Flowers standing at home plate with his hands on his hips.

But he didn't say anything. He just stepped on the plate, slapped hands with Jeremy, and ran toward the dugout. As he did, the coach walked over to meet him.

"What a blow," the coach said. "That was a perfect swing you took."

"Thanks," Thurlow said.

"The other players wanted to run out to home plate, but I stopped them. I told them not to show up the Mustangs this early in the game. No use making them mad." He grinned.

"That's right," Thurlow said. But the players were certainly ready for him when he reached the dugout. Everyone took turns slapping hands with him, telling him how great he was. And they looked a lot more confident now.

But Gloria got a good pitch and swung way too hard at it. She bounced it straight to the mound. Lou threw her out, and the inning was over.

Maybe Thurlow *was* going to have to win this game by himself today.

CHAPTER TWO

Thurlow hoped the Scrappers could settle down now. Maybe a two-run lead wasn't much, but it was a lot better than being behind in the score—and the way the Scrappers had played defense in the first inning, that could have happened.

Adam did look more relaxed. He threw a good fastball, just outside, and Alan Pingree reached for it and missed.

Thurlow could see that Pingree was pressing. He clearly didn't like the idea of the Scrappers having the lead. He wanted to do something about it.

But he swung hard at a change-up and pulled it foul down the left field line.

This was a big out, and Thurlow could see that Adam had his mind made up that he was going to get it. He nibbled on the outside corner with another fastball, but Pingree didn't bite this time. Then he tried a curveball that broke too low.

The noise picked up in the Mustangs' dugout. Snake Stabler, who was on deck, yelled, "This one's going to be in there, Al. *Smack* it!"

But Adam did the last thing Pingree expected. He changed up again, and Pingree triggered too soon.

Swish. Strike three.

Now it was the Scrappers who were screaming again.

Snake looked mad. He hustled to the plate and the dug in—like a bull getting ready to charge.

The first pitch was almost in the dirt, but Stabler swung at it and fouled it off. And then he chewed himself out. But when the next pitch came—another low one—he swung hard and knocked the ball on the grass, straight at Gloria.

Gloria had plenty of time, but she tried to scoop the ball without getting down. The ball glanced off the heel of her glove and hit her in the middle. She managed to grasp it against her body, but then she wrestled to get hold of it.

Her toss was high, but Ollie Allman, at first, stretched up and kept his foot on the bag.

It was close—but the ump called Stabler out.

Thurlow shook his head. What was Gloria doing? She was the best infielder on the team, and now she was looking like she was playing her first game.

But now there were two outs. If the Scrappers' luck could hold a little longer, if they could get out of this inning, maybe the players would settle down and play the way they could—and should.

Stein was up next—the kid everyone called "Gomer." The Mustangs didn't have any weak hitters. Even their pitchers could swing the bat. But Stein was one of the best. He watched a fastball go by outside. Then he waited on a curve. He took a quick, short swing, caught the ball solid, and drove it to left field.

Trent ran hard toward the line, but the ball got past him and rolled into the corner. He hurried, grabbed the ball, and made a good throw to Gloria at the cutoff spot. Gomer rounded second and held up.

Now Salinas was coming up. A big kid, who had some power, he was playing right field today. He could tie this game up if he got into one.

Adam knew that, too. So did Wilson. Wilson kept the target outside on the first two pitches, and Adam hit the spot. But Salinas didn't chase the ball, and Adam fell behind in the count, 2 and 0.

From that point, the battle was on. Salinas fouled off a couple, and then Adam threw one too low. Then, with the count full, Adam let a pitch get away from him. It took off high. Wilson came out of his crouch, reached up, and stopped the ball, but Salinas was on with a walk.

Flowers was up. He was a big swinger, so he struck out a lot, but he was another guy who could knock the hide off the ball.

Adam threw him a breaking ball, and Flowers swung for the fences. But he topped the ball and sent it scooting toward third base. It got to Robbie in a flash.

Robbie took a quick step to his left, reached out and snatched the ball on a low hop. All he had to do was tag third base.

But as he spun to do that, his feet gave way, and he went down. Then Thurlow saw the ball rolling across the dirt. Somehow, as Robbie had slipped, the ball had come out of his glove.

Robbie dove for the ball and got hold of it. But there just wasn't time to scramble to the bag before Stein got there. He slid in safe, and all the Mustangs' fans went crazy.

Robbie got up and turned away from Gomer. Thurlow was sure that the guy was telling Robbie what he thought of his brilliant play. Robbie stood with his hands on his hips and looked toward Gloria. She wasn't saying a word, and Thurlow knew why. She had messed up a play herself. Robbie just hadn't been quite so lucky as she had been.

From second base Tracy Matlock yelled to Robbie, "That's all right. We've got two outs. Take the easy one."

But she didn't sound her usual self. She seemed to be pleading more than showing her confidence.

Lou was coming up. He was the ninth batter in the lineup today, but the guy could hit, too. Thurlow thought about taking another step back, but he figured he could get back to the fence if he had to. He didn't want a ball to drop in front of him.

Thurlow's instinct was right. Lou swung at

the first pitch and sent a looping line drive straight up the middle. Thurlow flashed toward the infield and, at the last instant, dove for the ball. He was stretched all the way out when he felt the ball pop into his glove. He squeezed hard as his chest slammed into the ground.

Thurlow felt the air go out of him, but he rolled over fast and stood up—so the ump would see that he had the ball. The Scrappers had dodged a bullet. The Mustangs were retired, and they hadn't scored again.

Thurlow knew that he had taken a huge chance. If the ball had gotten past him, everyone might have scored. But he had been pretty sure the ball was within his reach. He hadn't really thought about it; he had just taken action. Something inside him was telling him that he could do no wrong today.

As he ran toward the dugout, Thurlow heard Alan Pingree yell, "Hey, Thurlow, you're a one-man team." That sounded like a compliment, but then Pingree added, "One guy's not going to beat us, though."

And that was right. Thurlow, for the first time, felt a little angry with his teammates.

They needed to pick it up, the way he was doing. That's what it was going to take to win this game.

But the Scrappers were still swinging their bats like a bunch of stiffs. They cheered for one another, got all psyched, and then walked out to the plate and took bad swings.

Trent struck out on a pitch over the heart of the plate. Then Tracy foul tipped a ball on a 2 and 2 count. Flowers hung on for the strikeout. Adam was next. He took a weak swing and poked the ball straight back to Lou.

One, two, three, and the Scrappers were back in the field.

Luckily, Adam was finding a groove. He got Mauer to pop up to Wilson, and then he fooled Donaldson, who swung late and bounced a little grounder to Tracy at second.

But Tracy got hold of the ball almost too soon. She tried to make a soft throw to first and aimed the ball too much. It flew wide of the bag and pulled Ollie off the base. Donaldson was safe.

But Adam didn't fuss about it. He kept his cool and struck out Gibby. Then he got Pingree on a high fly to left field. The Mustangs had been at bat three times, and the score was still 2 to 0.

When Thurlow got back to the bench, he felt like chewing the players out—telling them to settle down and start playing baseball. But that wasn't his style. Instead, he turned to Wilson and said, "Get on base next time. I'll get you home. We're going to need a big lead if we keep playing defense this way."

Wilson nodded. "All right," he said, but he sounded as nervous as the rest of them.

Ollie was leading off. He skipped a grounder to Pingree at first. Easy out.

Then Jeremy knocked another ground ball toward third.

Stein didn't charge the ball. He let it come to him, fielded it, and looked up to see Jeremy *flying* toward first. He threw hard and was on the money, but Jeremy zipped past the bag. "Safe!"

Mr. London was angry. "What are you doing out there?" he yelled at Stein. "That little kid can *run*. You know that."

Stein mumbled something, mostly to himself. He had to know that he had messed up.

Now Lou had a new worry: the little kid who could run was now leading off, looking for a chance to steal second. Lou seemed to pay more attention to Jeremy—who was taking a big lead—than to Robbie, the batter. He threw to first twice before he finally came with a pitch.

This time Robbie looked more like himself. He took a fluid swing, met the ball, and drove it over Stabler's head at short.

Gibby charged the ball from left field and got it back to the infield quickly. Jeremy had come hard around second, but he held up when he saw the coach raising his hands.

The Scrappers had something going, though, and Thurlow was going to get a chance to bat. He walked from the dugout, got his bat, and then knelt in the on-deck circle.

Thurlow watched Wilson take his strange, hunched-over stance. The big guy could unload on the ball sometimes, but in a tight moment he usually forgot everything he had learned.

On the first pitch, he swatted at the ball and missed. He laid off a low ball, but then he took another wild cut at a pitch that was up even with his eyes.

"Come on, Wilson," the coach yelled. "We don't need a homer. We just need to keep this inning going."

Wilson tried to take an easier swing on the next pitch, but he went after a ball that almost hit him, and he fouled it off the handle, right into Flowers's glove.

Strike three.

Now there were two outs, but Thurlow had runners on base, and that's what he had wanted.

As he walked to the plate, Wilson passed him. "Hey, man, I'm sorry," Wilson said. "It's up to you again."

"No problem."

And that's what Thurlow believed. He was in a zone. He just hoped that Lou would put the ball somewhere where he could get his bat on it.

Thurlow knew that Lou had a huge problem. There was no way he wanted to give Thurlow anything to hit, but he also didn't want to load the bases. Gloria, coming up next, wasn't so likely to knock the ball out of the park, but she could drive the ball hard and could easily clear the bases with an extra-base hit.

Mr. London called for a time-out and jogged to the mound. Flowers ran out, too, and some of the infielders walked over. There was a long discussion until the umpire finally broke it up, and everyone went back to their positions.

The park got very quiet. No one in the Mustangs' dugout was about to yell, "This guy can't hit." And the Scrappers were all waiting, just hoping Thurlow could bust another one.

Thurlow found it hard not to smile as he stood at the plate. "Just wait for your pitch," he kept whispering to himself. "Don't get too eager."

The first pitch was well outside, and Thurlow had to wonder what Lou had in mind. Maybe the Mustangs had decided to walk him after all—and take their chances with Gloria. The next pitch was closer, however, and Thurlow saw the plan: keep it out of his power zone and stay on the edge of the plate.

Thurlow wasn't going to try to pull an outside pitch—and certainly not chase a bad one. He would rather walk than hit something weak that would end the inning.

He moved a little closer to the plate and dared Lou to try to come inside.

The next pitch was slightly away—but closer than Lou probably wanted. Thurlow didn't try to pull it. He took an inside-out swing, caught the ball *flush*, and drove it hard to right field.

The ball took off like it might not get over the right fielder's head. But it didn't stop. It never got high in the air. It just kept going, and it disappeared over the fence.

Home run! A three-run shot!

The Scrappers were on top, 5 to 0.

Thurlow had taken off hard, but now he slowed down and went into his trot again. What he loved more than anything was the silence. Everyone was still looking to right field, like they couldn't believe anyone could hit the ball that hard.

Halfway around the bases, the noise did begin, and it kept mounting until he reached home plate. Coach Carlton hadn't been able to stop the Scrappers this time—or hadn't tried. The whole team was waiting for him at the plate.

Thurlow ran to them, accepted the high fives, but tried to get away quickly. He didn't want anyone to think the game was over. A five-run lead was great, but it might not be enough.

Gloria ended the inning with another ground-ball out—but the players did seem more relaxed. Coach Carlton yelled, "Now let's throw some leather at them," and Thurlow hoped that would happen.

CHAPTER THREE

The Mustangs looked like sleepwalkers. They yelled to one another that they could still win the game, but Thurlow saw little proof that they believed it. Part of their problem was that they had been so good early in the season that they hadn't had to improve. The other teams in the league had been catching up. Maybe the Scrappers had gotten a little lucky so far today, but the Mustangs had to know now that they couldn't take them lightly.

Still, Thurlow knew better than to get too confident. The Mustangs still had more pure talent than any team in the league. At any moment they could explode and pick up a bunch of runs *fast*.

As it turned out, however, the Scrappers didn't have to play good defense in the fourth inning. The Mustangs were almost frantic to get something going. They were swinging recklessly, and Adam was *popping* the ball. He struck out Stabler on a high fastball, and then he caught Stein looking at a third strike.

Mr. London was losing his cool. "What are you taking a pitch like that for?" he yelled at Gomer. "With two strikes, you've got to be ready." Just a moment before he had been yelling at the kid for swinging at a bad pitch.

Salinas came up, swung for the fence, and lifted a high pop-up to the right side of the diamond. Wilson and Ollie both went after it, but Ollie called Wilson off and took it himself, right up against the fence.

That was a good sign. Thurlow breathed a little easier. *If* Adam kept throwing like that . . . and *if* the Mustangs kept struggling at the plate . . . and *if* the Scrappers could make some plays, maybe everything would come out all right. One thing he knew for sure was that *he* was going to keep driving in runs.

The bottom of the fourth started well. Trent worked Lou to a 3 and 1 count, then stroked a fastball into left field. It was a good at bat from Trent, one of the players who needed to come through. But Tracy hit a grounder to second, and

Billy Mauer threw to Stabler for the force at second. Then Adam popped the ball up, and big Flowers made the catch for the second out.

Thurlow wasn't about to start yelling and cheering, but he did tell Ollie, "Come on. Keep the inning going. We need to build our lead."

Ollie tried, too. He took a couple of pitches for balls, and then he got a terrible call from the ump. The pitch was down, just above Ollie's ankles, but the umpire called it a strike. Ollie didn't complain, but the call seemed to upset him. He ended up striking out, and the side was retired.

The fifth inning went the same way. Flowers got hold of one of Adam's fastballs and drove it down the line in right. By the time Jeremy could run it down, Flowers had a double. But he ended up stranded there. Lou and Mauer both hit fly balls to Trent in left, and then Donaldson struck out on a big-breaking curveball.

"No way, ump," Donaldson said. "That ball was outside." But he didn't sound like he believed it.

Thurlow sensed that the Mustangs believed they were beaten. They were trying to fire themselves up, show some fight, but Adam had them under control, and that five-run lead was looking bigger all the time.

But Jeremy, Robbie, and Wilson went down one-two-three in the bottom of the fifth, and Thurlow didn't get his chance at bat. He had wanted to nail one more, with someone on base, and put the game away.

Six more outs—that's what the Scrappers needed. But the excitement of Thurlow's big shot in the third inning was over, and the Scrappers were yelling less and less. Thurlow knew what everyone was thinking: "We can't mess up. We can't blow this game now that we've come this far."

Thurlow thought he even saw Adam pressing a little too hard on his warm-up pitches before the sixth inning started. "Hey, Adam," Thurlow yelled, and he ran toward the infield.

Adam turned around. "You're doing great. Don't start overthrowing. Just stay with your good motion."

"Okay," Adam said.

But Thurlow heard the nervousness in his voice. He wished he hadn't said anything.

The Scrappers did pick up their chatter. But so did the Mustangs.

Gibby was up. This could be the last at bat

for her, and she was looking serious. She was one who hadn't given up on the game—that was for sure.

Gibby swung and missed on Adam's first pitch, a fastball, and Thurlow was relieved to see the ball in a great spot, down and away, on the edge of the plate.

But Adam came back with a curveball, and Gibby stayed with it. She punched it toward the right side, over Cindy Jones, who was now playing second for Tracy.

So Gibby had a leadoff single, and the Mustangs came alive. The players were all standing up in the dugout, and they were really working on Adam. As Pingree walked to the plate, they were yelling, "Keep it going, Al. Adam's arm is shot. He's lost his stuff."

Pingree got cocked and ready. When Adam fired a fastball over the plate, he exploded. He lashed a line drive toward right field. It was a hard shot, but Cindy reacted. She stepped to her left and leaped, her arm stretching across her body.

It happened in an instant, but the ball hit her glove . . . and stuck like it was glued there.

It was a great catch—maybe the best Cindy had ever made. She came down off balance and dropped to her knees. If she had stayed up, she might have doubled Gibby off first.

The air seemed to go out of the Mustangs, and the Scrappers' confidence took a huge surge.

Stabler struck out on three pitches. Then Stein hit a high, lazy fly ball to center, and Thurlow smiled. He trotted in a few steps and made the grab with one hand.

He was coming up first in the bottom of the sixth, probably his last time at bat. He told himself he didn't need to hit another homer. But it would be fun to get three in one game.

He waited for Lou to throw his warm-up pitches, then walked to the plate as the Scrappers' fans sent up a roar. "Park one, Thurlow!" he heard people yelling. "Lose another one."

But his coach and his mom were saying, "Just meet the ball, Thurlow. Let's get something going."

Lou wasn't going to give him anything he could pull—that was for sure. The first pitch was way outside. Maybe the coach had told him to bait Thurlow but not throw him anything he could hit.

That was understandable, but Thurlow didn't want to walk. He wanted another hit. He moved in close to the plate again, and then he reached for an outside pitch and fouled it off.

"That was ball two, Thurlow," Coach Carlton called. "Don't make it easy on the guy. Take the walk, if that's what he wants to give you."

But the next pitch was over the plate. Thurlow met the ball solid. It snapped off his bat and darted, like a rope, down the right field line. It was hit too low to get out of the park, but it was past the right fielder in an instant and rolling all the way to the corner of the field.

Thurlow knew he had a triple as soon as he saw where the ball was heading, but he was thinking inside-the-park homer. Salinas, playing right, was not very fast. He had a good arm, but it was going to take a great relay to get Thurlow.

So Thurlow burned around first and went all out for second. He looped out as he approached second, and came at the bag with his right foot, ready to tag the base and launch himself toward third.

As his foot hit the bag, he looked toward Coach Carlton, and he wondered whether the coach would give him the green light. But just then, something gave way.

Thurlow felt pain—like an electrical shock—shoot through his ankle. He tumbled to the ground and rolled. The pain was so bad he could hardly think of anything else. But he didn't forget what he had to do. As soon as he could roll over, he did, and then he scurried on his hands and knees back to second. He slapped his hand on the bag, and then he gasped, "Time-out! Time-out!"

He didn't want to act like a baby, didn't want to scream or cry, but he had never felt such pain. He rolled up in a ball and grasped his arms around his knee. Then he sucked in all the breath he could get and held it in, hoping the worst of the agony might pass before long.

His mother was there by then, as well as Coach Carlton. Their faces were above him. "How bad is it?" his mom wanted to know.

Thurlow couldn't answer, didn't know what he would say if he could. He just wanted the pain to stop.

"Your foot seemed to catch against the bag," Coach Carlton said. "You rolled your ankle really bad."

An umpire was there now, and then the other

Scrappers started showing up. A lot of people were saying things. Thurlow shut his eyes and tried to block it all out. He just wanted the hurt to stop.

Then he heard someone say, "I wonder if it's broken."

"No!" Thurlow yelled, but he didn't really know whether his ankle was broken or not. He just didn't want to accept the idea that that was possible. However much his ankle hurt, the worst thing he could think of was that his season would end out here on the ground—when the Scrappers needed to finish off this game and then win one more.

"This is Tracy's dad," Thurlow heard the coach say. "He's a doctor."

Thurlow had seen Dr. Matlock before. But he didn't want to see him now. "It's not broken," he said. "I'll be all right in a minute. It's just—"

"Stay still." Dr. Matlock took hold of Thurlow's foot. When he moved it, pain shot up Thurlow's leg. "Does that hurt?" the doctor asked.

"No," Thurlow answered, but his grunt had already said more than his denial could.

"We need to get you over to the hospital and

get an X ray," Dr. Matlock said. Then he said to the coach, "Give me some help here. Let's get him off the field."

The two of them hoisted Thurlow off the ground and lifted him between the two of them, in a basket carry. Now Thurlow's leg was hanging down, and every step the men took sent shock waves clear to his knee. Still, he was pleading, "Don't take me to the hospital yet. Let me watch the rest of the game."

"Well . . . all right," the doctor said. "Let's let him sit on the bench. It won't hurt to let him watch this last inning. But we need to get some ice on it right away."

So they put Thurlow on the bench, and Dr. Matlock pulled his shoe off. Thurlow finally looked down to see that the ankle was already swollen—full and round where he had once been able to see his anklebone. He glanced around to see his teammates gathered as close as they could get, all of them looking shaken and worried. Even the crowd was standing, silent, looking toward the dugout.

"We need a batter out here," the umpire finally yelled.

"All right, we've got a game to finish," Coach

said. "Chad, you go run for Thurlow. Let's get this run in."

But the life had gone out of the team. Gloria tried to make something happen, but she swung through a couple of pitches, got mad at herself, and then took a called strike for the out. Then Trent hit an easy roller to second base, and Cindy got under a pitch and raised a high fly to left.

Chad ended up stranded at second.

But that wasn't the important thing. The Scrappers needed three outs. Thurlow just hoped the players would keep their heads in the game.

"Hey, kids," the coach yelled. "Don't you dare go out on that field looking like a bunch of zombies. You get out there and *play ball*. Thurlow was giving it everything he had when he went down. Now you do the same thing. Let's get those last three outs."

A cheer went up, and that sounded good. But Thurlow wondered what would happen on the field.

CHAPTER FOUR

Wanda got some ice from the concession stand behind the bleachers. As the Scrappers got ready to play defense, she dumped the ice on a towel, folded it, and then wrapped the towel around Thurlow's ankle. That hurt—plenty—but Thurlow didn't want to say so.

"Thurlow," his mom said, "you're squirming and making faces. I know that ankle is killing you. I think we'd better get to the hospital right now."

"No. I've got to see this. It's just half an inning."

Gloria was shouting, "Here we go, Scrappers. Fire that ball, Adam." Thurlow knew she was trying to take charge, bring the team back to life.

Salinas was up, and it was pretty clear he wasn't looking to hammer the ball. The Mustangs needed base runners. Salinas took a ball, outside, but then he let one go by at the knees, and the ump called it a strike. "No way!" he said, and he slammed his bat on home plate.

But he didn't fuss long. He set up ready again, and this time, when Adam put another one across the plate, Salinas took a short, quick swing and jabbed the ball to right field.

It was a sinking fly ball, but Thurlow was sure that Jeremy could handle it. And then he remembered. The coach had sent Jeremy to center. Chad was in right field.

Chad charged hard, but he just wasn't very fast. At the last second he pulled up and tried to take the ball on one hop, but it bounced high, and it got by him.

Jeremy had been running hard to back up Chad. He chased the ball down and threw to second, but Salinas slid under Gloria's tag, safe.

Gloria smacked the ball into her glove a couple of times, and then she tossed it to Adam. Thurlow knew she was mad—that she wanted to chew out Chad. But this was no time to start that kind of stuff. "That's all right, Chad," Thurlow shouted. "They need five runs. That guy on second doesn't mean a thing."

Thurlow was no cheerleader, but he didn't know what else he could do now. The team needed to know he was still with them.

What worried him now was that the Mustangs were really rocking over in their dugout— shouting and going nuts. And they had reason to think they could score now. Not only were Chad and Cindy in the game, but Martin Epting was in for Trent. The outfield was anything but strong now.

Flowers was up, with Lou after him. Neither of them were consistently good hitters, but Flowers could really make the ball soar a mile when he connected well, and Lou had very good bat control. Adam had to be looking for a strike out, not wanting Flowers to get a chance to knock himself and Salinas in—and not wanting to give Chad or Martin a chance to mess up.

Adam gunned a fastball, but it stayed high. And then he put another one in the same spot. Now the Mustangs were all over Adam. "He's losing his cool, Brandon," Pingree shouted. "He's going to walk you."

Adam took a long breath and let it out, and then he brought the ball down. Way down. Ball three.

Thurlow didn't want to watch. His ankle was throbbing, and maybe his own season was down the drain, but he had given everything to this game, and he wanted this win. The second-half championship was at least something, even if the Scrappers couldn't take it all.

Adam tossed a pitch down the middle with little on it, but Flowers was taking it all the way. He missed. Now the count was 3 and 1, but Adam had to throw another strike without making it as fat as that last pitch.

It took some guts to try a curve at that point, but he did, and he got it over. Flowers took it for strike two.

Full count. The crowd and the players were all yelling back and forth, and then, as Adam took his sign, everything got silent. Adam threw a lightning bolt down the middle—and Flowers didn't swing.

Adam pumped his arm and said, "Yes!"

But Thurlow saw it before Adam did. The ump had called the pitch ball four. He was sending Flowers to first.

Wilson spun all the way around. "What?!" he shouted into the umpire's face. "That was perfect! What were you looking at?"

Coach Carlton ran toward the plate. "Wilson, that's enough," he said. But then he asked the umpire, "Where was it? It looked awfully good."

"Outside," the ump said, but he didn't sound very sure of himself. Thurlow couldn't believe it. The ump had blown a major call at the worst possible time.

Wilson was arguing again, but Coach told him, "Turn around, Wilson. Play ball."

Now the Mustangs were building the noise, and so were their fans. The momentum of the game was swinging. Thurlow felt a disaster coming. He wanted to be out there on that field. He wanted to get something done. And all he could do was yell. "That's all right. Don't worry about the runners. All we need is three outs."

Robbie looked at Gloria. "Take two if you can," he yelled, "but get the sure one."

She socked her glove, and then she yelled the same thing to Cindy.

Lou was up now—he wasn't very fast. He was an easy guy to double up if he hit the ball on the ground. Thurlow tried not to think about his strength.

Lou didn't try to work Adam. He saw a pitch he liked, and he took a big swing. But he topped the ball and sent it scooting toward Gloria.

And Gloria was ready. The ball flattened out,

but she stayed with it. She took it on a flat bounce, gloved it clean, and came up ready to throw to second.

But then she had to double pump . . . and wait.

Cindy was late getting to the bag.

Gloria finally threw, but her timing was off, and she didn't have much on the ball. Cindy made a good catch and tagged the base in time, but any chance for a double play was gone.

"What were you doing over there?" Gloria screamed at Cindy.

Cindy didn't answer. She turned and walked away. Thurlow had no explanation. Cindy had made a great catch in the sixth inning, and now she had gone to sleep just when she should have been ready to make a play.

At least they had gotten the force-out.

"All right, we only need two," Thurlow yelled.

Gloria nodded. And then she called to Cindy, "Don't worry about it. We got the important one."

Thurlow knew that Gloria didn't want to mess up this game right now—not with her glove, and not with her mouth. She had done that too many times this season.

There were runners on first and third now, but Salinas, on third, didn't matter. The Scrappers would trade a run for an out, and be glad to have it.

The top of the batting order was coming up—and lots of speed. Someone was going to have to make a play for the Scrappers.

Mauer stepped up as the crowd kept up the noise. Thurlow's foot wasn't so bad if he sat absolutely still, but he couldn't seem to do that. Each time he shouted to his teammates or waved his fist, the movement sent pain charging up his leg.

Adam was taking more time now, but he didn't seem rattled. He tried to hit the outer edge and missed a couple of times, but he got the next pitch over the plate. Mauer took a good swing but didn't connect very well.

The ball arced toward left field. Gloria turned her back and ran all out, chasing it. Martin was running hard from the outfield. But neither one could get there in time.

Gloria grabbed the ball on one bounce, spun,

and threw a rope to home plate. Salinas, on third, had had to wait to see whether anyone would catch the ball. He had played it halfway, but now he had to hustle back to third.

So the bases were loaded. This whole thing could break wide open now. And nothing seemed to be going right. If Trent had been in left, he probably would have gotten a better jump and would have caught that last one.

Thurlow had never felt this much tension. The Scrappers were all silent now, except for Trent and Tracy, who were on the bench with him. What Thurlow sensed was the fear in all the players on the field.

Even Adam looked like he was beginning to believe nothing was ever going to go right again. He paced off the mound, seemed to look inside himself for some inner toughness, and then went back to the rubber.

He threw a pitch that was up a little, and Donaldson couldn't resist. He took a hard swing and popped it up. Cindy probably should have taken it, but Adam pointed to the ball and yelled, "Gloria." She moved past the base at second, got under the ball, and made the catch.

A huge sigh came out of the crowd. The Scrappers' supporters seemed to be gasping, letting off steam.

Thurlow was breathing again. "Okay, just one more. Take the easy one." Then he let out a little grunt of pain.

"Sit still," his mother told him, but she started screaming herself and set the bench jiggling. That hurt, too.

The Mustangs usually had more subs in the game by now. But they had put only one in today, so Gibby was still coming up. She would get one more chance after all, and she wasn't one to get too impatient either. She was a great line-drive hitter.

She took a ball, up, but then Adam came with a wicked fastball at the knees. Gibby stroked it toward Robbie at third.

It was hit like a missile, and it got to Robbie on one skidding bounce. He stayed in front of it, but it skipped off his glove and bounced off his chest. He scrambled after it, grabbed it, and then he spun and dove for third. He tagged the base just as Lou was hook sliding into the bag.

Dirt flew, and for a moment, Thurlow didn't

know. And then the umpire shouted, "Out!"

The game was over!

The Scrappers had done it.

They came charging off the field, leaping and shouting, and then they charged towards each other. They jumped in the air, banged chests, and knocked one another around. And then they headed for Thurlow.

But Wanda was shouting, "Don't come too close. He's in a lot of pain."

"Go shake hands with the Mustangs," Coach Carlton was shouting, "and then I want to talk to you."

So the players yelled to Thurlow, but they didn't come close. Then they ran back on the field and lined up. The Mustangs didn't have the big mouths that some of the teams did, but they were certainly not enjoying this.

Thurlow was watching when he saw Gloria, without warning, suddenly give Mauer a shove. Tracy grabbed her immediately and pulled her away. The two of them broke off from the line, and Gloria stalked back toward the dugout. "I'm sorry, Coach," she said, "but Mauer told me, 'You guys have no chance next time. You're a one-man team, and your man is gone.'"

"Never mind. Just come over here," Coach said.

So the kids gathered around, close to the entrance to the dugout.

"Listen, kids," Coach Carlton said. "I talked to Dr. Matlock. He doesn't think Thurlow's foot is broken, but it might be. And even if it isn't, there's really no chance that he can play in a week."

Thurlow knew what everyone was thinking. He knew what *he* was thinking. The Scrappers couldn't win without him.

"The first thing we've got to do is get Thurlow to the hospital. Then we need to practice hard this week. We're a good team. We're *not* a one-man team. Thurlow is a great player, but you're all good, and we can beat the Mustangs again."

But no one cheered. Everyone just stood there—even the parents—and the silence said it all.

CHAPTER FIVE

Thurlow was lying on his back on a hard table. He was in a quiet little room without much light. He heard a clicking sound, and then the nurse walked back into the room. "Okay, that was the last X ray," she said. "I won't have to twist you around any more."

"When will I know how bad it is?" Thurlow asked.

"It won't be long. In a few minutes an orderly will be here. He'll get you into a wheelchair and take you back to the emergency room. Then the doctor will come and talk to you."

"It doesn't hurt as bad as it did at first."

"Well, that's good. But you can't really tell what's going on until the doctor takes a close look."

She put a blanket over Thurlow and left the room. With air-conditioning, the room was sort of cool, but he didn't want to be treated like he was sick. At least the doctor had let him leave his uniform on. One of the nurses had wanted him to get into one of those dumb little nightgown things—with the wide-open back. Thurlow had told the nurse, "No way. It's just my ankle," and the doctor had walked in then and agreed with him.

But now, lying in this darkened little room, he had time to think. He wondered whether his ankle was messed up bad. Maybe it was broken, or maybe the ligaments were torn. He could end up in a cast for a while, and that could mean not only the end of his baseball season but maybe his football season, too. His mom had already brought that up, and it made him mad that she would start thinking that way already.

"All I'm saying is, you can't do anything with it too soon, and injure it forever," she had told him. It wasn't that she was wrong, but his mother was always too careful about everything. That was part of the reason the two of them struggled with each other.

At the beginning of the summer Thurlow had decided he wasn't going to play baseball. His best friends weren't playing, and they had planned to work on their basketball all summer so they could make the junior high team together. There was nothing wrong with that. Sometimes a guy had to specialize, pick one or two sports and not try to play them all.

The only trouble was, his mom didn't like Thurlow's friends; she thought they were a "bad influence" on him. That was the reason she had been so insistent that he play baseball. She liked Wilson and Robbie and some of the other kids on the Scrappers—and she had wanted Thurlow to hang out with them instead of his real buddies.

So Thurlow had done a slow burn in the beginning. He'd felt forced on to a team that just wasn't that good, and he hadn't liked some of the players—especially Gloria. He had never expected to become as committed to the team as he now was. But he couldn't help liking the coach, and the Scrappers just kept getting better. And something in Thurlow always said, "I won't finish second."

So now the team was right there. The Scrappers had their chance to win the whole thing, and then this happens—a stupid injury.

How could he have tripped over the dumb bag, just rounding a base?

What bothered him as much as anything was that he had been having a day never to forget. Two homers and those great catches in center field. The Scrappers could have taken that momentum into the championship game and blown away the Mustangs. But now . . . what chance did they have?

Thurlow felt sorry for all the players. He knew how down they had to be. It almost seemed sad that they would have to play their last game under the lights in the big park at the college. He hoped they wouldn't end up looking really bad. Chad would have to start—and this time Salinas would be pitching.

What a mess.

Then he heard voices in the hallway—voices he knew. Wilson and Robbie and Trent. He wasn't exactly surprised. What did surprise him was how glad he was. At the first of the season he had tried to avoid these guys. Now he was happy they had come over.

He was hearing some of the other players, too, and then the door opened and all of them came in. "The nurse told us where you were,"

Robbie said. "She said we could come in and see you for a minute."

"Hey," Thurlow said, and he raised his head. Every player was there, and they were all crowding around the table.

"Is it broken?" Wilson asked.

"I don't know. The doctor has to look at it, and then he'll let me know. Even if it isn't, he said I couldn't play in the last game."

"I know."

But that hadn't sounded right. Wilson didn't seem all that broken up about it. "If I can play . . . if there's any way at all, I will."

"Naw," Trent said, "you can't do that. You need to stay off it and make sure it heals right. You don't want to hurt it any worse."

Gloria was standing behind Cindy. She leaned to one side and said, "That's right, Thurlow. But don't worry. We talked it over. We played lousy today, but we're going in loose next time—and we're going to get those guys."

"All right. Great," Thurlow said, but he couldn't believe it. The Scrappers didn't have a chance without him there. Gloria was kidding herself.

"Boy, you have an ugly foot," Ollie said. He sounded serious, but sort of distant—the way he often did.

"I know. It's really swollen," Thurlow said.

"No. I mean your toes. You have long bony toes."

Everyone cracked up—and made way too much noise. But Thurlow didn't think it was all that funny. For one thing, the kids were bumping the table, sending painful vibrations through his ankle.

"Be careful," Thurlow said, but no one seemed to hear him. They were all talking and laughing with one another.

"Robbie, that was a close call on that last play," Thurlow finally said. "If Lou had been safe, I hate to think what might have happened." Thurlow laughed a little, but the truth was, he wanted to remind all the kids that they had come within a few inches of blowing the game. How did they think they were going to take the next one?

"Yeah, I know," Robbie said. "But we had a big lead. One run would have scored if he'd been safe, but we still had two outs on them.

We wouldn't have given up *five* runs."

Adam grinned. "Hey, I wanted that shutout," he said.

Thurlow couldn't believe these kids. They had been out there on that field, scared half to death, and now they were talking like they had had no problems. Someone needed to remind them how they got that five-run lead—and who made all the big catches in the outfield.

Over all the voices, Thurlow heard the nurse. "Okay, kids. That's enough. You said you were going to be quiet, and you're making enough noise to wake up the whole hospital."

"We'll quiet down," Martin said.

"No. It's time to go. I've got an orderly out here who wants to take Thurlow back to his room in the ER."

"Oooh, the *ER*," Wilson said. "Hey, Thurlow, they'll put those electric things on your chest and shoot the juice into you."

Tracy laughed hard. "Yeah. And they'll stick a bunch of tubes down your nose. It could get ugly around here."

Meanwhile, out in the hallway, the big joke was Thurlow's wheelchair. "Thurlow's limo is here," Gloria said, loud enough to break cracks in the walls.

Chad had apparently sat down in the thing. Thurlow heard the orderly say, "Okay, I need that now," and Jeremy told him, "Hey, I was going to give Chad a ride down the hall."

They were having a great time, and Thurlow was starting to get tired of it. But then Trent stepped back to the X-ray table. "You played the greatest game I've ever seen, Thurlow. That's really why we came over here—to thank you for everything. Man, without you, we never would have made it to this point."

"That's right," Robbie said. "You did it pretty much by yourself today. But this next game, we're going to do it *for* you. We're not going to let the championship get away, now that we've got a shot."

Thurlow couldn't be mad, not after that.

When he got back to the emergency room his mother made him get back on the bed, and then she elevated his foot with a pillow. Thurlow didn't want to hear all her instructions about staying home, using crutches, and keeping his weight off the foot. He kept his mouth shut, and finally she got the hint, and she quieted, too.

When the doctor finally showed up, he was smiling. "Well, son, it's not all that bad," he said. "There's no break and no serious ligament damage. It's just a matter of icing it and staying off it for a while. It'll heal pretty fast. You'll be surprised."

"You mean, I could still play in the game next week?"

"No, no. I don't think so. It won't come around that fast, and it wouldn't be wise to take any chances that soon. But in two or three weeks, it should be pretty much back to normal."

"Does he need crutches or a cast or anything?" Wanda asked.

"I'll put a soft cast on it—one he can take off when he showers. But he won't need crutches. For the next forty-eight hours he shouldn't put much weight on it, but after that, he can start to walk—you know, a little at a time."

All this was good news, in a way. But it drove Thurlow nuts to think that if he only had a little more time he might be able to play.

The doctor left and came back with a black cast, which he carefully placed on Thurlow's foot and pulled tight with Velcro fasteners. Then he told Thurlow he could go. Thurlow got back in the wheelchair, and the orderly wheeled him out to the emergency entrance. While his mom was getting her car, the coach finally showed up. "Thurlow, I'm glad I got here before you left. What did the doctors tell you?"

"It's not broken. It'll be all right in a couple of weeks."

"Oh, good. That's great news."

"Not that great. I can't play next week."

"Oh, I knew that when I first looked at it."

"I'm sorry I made a mess of things."

"Hey, it was just one of those things that can happen. But the kids think they can still win, and I wouldn't put it past them. They're going to be aggressive this time—not play like they're scared of getting beat."

Thurlow nodded. "Well, yeah," he said. "Maybe they can do it."

But he didn't really think so. And what he wished was that the coach, just between the two of them, would admit that he didn't think so either.

CHAPTER SIX

The Scrappers were lined up along the third base line. They were holding their caps over their hearts, and they were looking out toward center field, where a big American flag was stirring in the evening breeze. The championship game was about to begin on the big college field, and it was exciting.

Thurlow was standing in line with the others, even wearing his uniform, but he had sandals on his feet. For the last two days he had argued that he could play, that his ankle didn't hurt all that much anymore, and that if he wrapped it well enough . . .

But the argument hadn't made a dent in his mother's position. "You know what the doctor told you," she kept saying. "If you try to play on it too soon, you could really make things worse."

The trouble was, Coach Carlton agreed. "We

want to win, Thurlow," he told him before the game, "and I'd love to have you out there tonight. But I won't take the chance of ruining your future in sports."

So when the "Star-Spangled Banner" ended, and the crowd cheered, Thurlow walked back to the dugout. The Scrappers had won the coin toss and were playing as the home team, so the Mustangs would bat first.

The stadium could handle four or five times as many people as the park downtown could, but the place was nearly full. All the parents were there, along with the usual friends and supporters. But in addition, there were a lot of people from Wasatch City who hadn't seen a game all year. It was really the place to be tonight. Even a lot of the teenagers from around town were there.

Thurlow kept thinking what he could have done on a night like this, in front of such a big crowd. The fences were farther back than in the city recreation park, but that didn't bother Thurlow. He could have pounded the ball over the fence anyway, and that would have been even more fun. He also could have made longer runs to catch fly balls in deep center.

It would have been his night.

Instead, he had to head for the dugout—a *real* dugout. He sat down on the steps. From there, he could see the whole field, and he could watch the coach give his signals.

Coach Carlton walked over to him. "Help me think through this game tonight, Thurlow," he said. "You have a good head for baseball. If you notice anything I ought to be aware of, let me know. I might ask you what you think about some of the decisions I'll have to make."

Thurlow liked that. He could tell the coach was serious, not just trying to make him feel part of the game. Still, Thurlow didn't think the Scrappers had much of a chance. They were acting confident, but he worried that once things didn't go their way, they might fall apart.

Thurlow watched Ollie as he warmed up. He had a strange look in his eyes. He seemed to be floating in space somewhere, his mind not really in the here and now. But he wasn't talking to himself and didn't look concerned. He was firing pure heat and getting everything over the plate.

When Mauer stepped up to bat, an announcer's voice boomed through the stadium: "Ladies and gentlemen, batting first for the

Mustangs will be Billy Mauer." The sound reverberated across the field and out into the night. This felt like the big time, and Thurlow could hardly stand it. He wanted to be out there in center, ready for that first fly ball to come his way.

Ollie didn't waste a lot of time. He took his signal from Wilson, wound up, and chucked a bomb of a fastball right over the plate. Mauer let it go by for a strike.

Ollie got the ball back and was ready to go again. No chatting with himself tonight. He tossed another good fastball, this one down in the strike zone. Mauer spanked it hard on the ground toward third base.

It seemed headed past Robbie into left field, but he dove to his left and knocked it down. Then, just as quickly, he was up and on it. He grabbed the ball, set his feet, and tossed a laser beam of a throw to Adam at first.

Out!

It was a fancy play, and the big crowd gave Robbie a loud cheer.

The Scrappers seemed to feed off the energy. They were all yelling to one another, talking it up. Ollie pumped a couple of steamers past

Eddie Donaldson, wasted one outside, and then struck him out on a curveball.

The Scrappers picked up their chatter, even louder, and the crowd was already into the game. Big Mr. Gibbs, Gloria's dad, bellowed, "That's the stuff, kids. We got 'em tonight."

Sheri Gibby came up next. She drove the ball rather hard to center field. Jeremy ran back, angling to his left, circled under the ball, and then waited. He made the catch, and the top of the inning was over.

Coach Carlton was clapping and shouting as his team came off the field. "You look great out there, kids," he told them. "Like major-leaguers."

"That's right," Thurlow told them. He gave everyone a hand slap as his teammates came past him down the dugout steps.

When Thurlow's mom came into the dugout, she told him, "Now be careful. You ought to sit down on the bench, where no one will bump into you."

"Come on, Mom. I'm fine."

She shrugged and let it go. "They looked great, didn't they?" she said.

"Yeah. I just hope they can keep it up."

"What do you mean?"

"Nothing. Just what I said."

"Thurlow, this is a good team."

"I know it is."

She rolled her eyes and then walked to the other end of the dugout. But Thurlow knew exactly what she was thinking. She always told him that he hadn't become part of the team, that he wasn't really friends with the other players. Now she was accusing him—with that look of hers—of having no faith in them. But she was forgetting how bad the Scrappers could be at times.

Thurlow *had* changed his attitude a lot this summer. His mom wasn't giving him enough credit for that, and it made him mad. He went back to his usual silence. And he thought, *Just wait until they need a big hit and there's no one out there who can get it. That's when Mom will quit talking about how good they are.*

Salinas was throwing some flames of his own. He looked tough. But he had trouble finding Jeremy's strike zone, and Jeremy worked him for a walk.

That was a great start, but Robbie hit a sharp grounder to Stabler, who gobbled it up and flipped it to Mauer at second, who made the pivot and fired to Pingree at first. Double play.

The good start was erased.

And then Gloria hit a fly ball to left, and now it was the Mustangs who looked like big leaguers. This was going to be a battle tonight.

Alan Pingree led off the top of the second inning. Ollie made a perfect pitch—on the inside corner of the plate at the knees—but Pingree reached down and muscled it into left field for a single. The guy was a great hitter.

Ollie didn't seem ruffled, but he got a little too fine with Stabler. The Mustangs' shortstop fouled a couple off, worked the count to 3 and 2, fouled another one, and then finally walked.

This was the first threat of the game, and Thurlow wondered how the Scrappers would handle it. He glanced at his mother, but she wouldn't look his way.

The Mustangs' supporters were making a lot of noise as Gomer Stein walked to the plate. But Chad's dad, Mr. Corrigan, was louder than any of them. "No problem. You can get this guy, Ollie," he was yelling. Maybe he had made up his mind not to embarrass his son the way he had sometimes in the past—and be a supporter.

But Stein *was* a problem. He swung at the first pitch and hit a long shot to center. Jeremy dropped back fast, but the ball was over his head. It bounced ahead of him, and he kept chasing it, but Thurlow could see that two runs would probably score. Jeremy had great speed but not much of an arm.

Still, the Scrappers knew what to do. They had practiced these situations. Gloria raced into shallow center to the cutoff position, and Tracy covered her base at second. Jeremy got to the ball, turned, and hit Gloria right on the money. Gloria turned and *gunned* the ball home.

Pingree had scored, but Wilson was set up perfectly for Stabler. He blocked the plate and got his glove down. Stabler tried to slide through him, but he didn't have a chance. Wilson put the tag on him for the out.

Stein cruised into third on the throw, but things could have been worse. The Scrappers had handled the ball perfectly and cut off one of the runs.

Of course, Thurlow had to wonder what might have happened had he been in center field. Jeremy was fast, but Thurlow was faster. He was pretty sure that he could have made that catch and that the Scrappers wouldn't have given up *any* runs. The difference—not having him out there—was starting to show.

But Ollie didn't seem upset. He threw a couple of good fastballs for strikes, and then he changed up. Salinas was fooled, and he went down swinging. Next up tonight was Justin Lou, who was playing right field, and he hit a fly ball to right. Thurlow held his breath, but Chad came in a few steps and made the catch. The Scrappers had given up a run, but they hadn't fallen apart. Thurlow had to give them credit for that.

This inning would have been Thurlow's time to come up to bat. Maybe he could have gotten back that run with a long shot over the fence.

Instead, Wilson struck out on a curveball. And then Trent and Tracy were both overpowered—and they struck out, too.

Salinas was throwing pure heat. It was hard to believe the Scrappers were going to get a lot of runs tonight, the way he had it going. They had to keep playing great defense to have any chance. And with Chad out there in right, Thurlow had to wonder when his first big mistake would happen.

Flowers led off the third with a double. And

then Mauer slapped a grounder to the right side. The ball seemed headed for right field, but Tracy made a beautiful play on the ball. She made the stop, spun, and threw to Adam, who got Mauer on a close call.

Tracy's play had saved another run, but now Flowers was on third with only one out.

Ollie threw a great curveball that caught Donaldson off balance. But he managed to flare a little fly ball into right. Chad came up for it, took it on one bounce, and Flowers scored.

It was luck. Pure luck. Donaldson had barely made contact, but he had an RBI to show for it.

Maybe it would have been a run anyway, even if Jeremy had been in right instead of Chad. But Thurlow had to wonder.

In any case, the score was now 2 to 0. The Scrappers just couldn't let it get any worse.

When Gibby hit a hard grounder down the first base line, Thurlow's breath caught. But Adam made a great stop, and then, instead of taking the sure out at first, he pulled off the play the Scrappers had practiced all summer. He threw to Tracy at second, and she relayed the ball back to Adam. Double play—the hard way!

It was the toughest double play for an infield

to make, first to second and back to first, but the Scrappers had made it look easy. They were keeping the game close.

As Mr. London walked to the third base coach's box, he looked into the dugout. The Scrappers were all just getting to the bench. "Hey, kids, that was a fine play. You've got quite a team. I've never seen a bunch of kids improve as much in one year as you have."

"Thanks, Coach," Trent said, but as soon as Mr. London walked on, Trent looked at the other players. "But we didn't come here just to look good. We came to win!"

All the players shouted, "Yeah," "That's right," and "Let's get some runs now."

But Thurlow was watching Salinas pump the ball as he took his warm-up pitches. The guy was scary.

CHAPTER SEVEN

Adam was up first in the bottom of the third. He got behind in the count, 1 and 2, but then he at least got a piece of the ball. He lifted a pop-up to the left side. Stabler got under it and made the catch.

Thurlow could see another three-up/three-down inning coming.

Salinas threw a couple of fastballs by Ollie, and he looked to be in deep trouble. But then Salinas changed up, and Ollie finally got his bat around on a pitch. He hit a high bouncer toward Stein at third.

Gomer got caught between hops and had to leap high to glove the ball. When he landed, he tried to hurry, and he didn't get the ball out of his glove with the first grab. When he did get the throw away, he really blasted it, but

Ollie was galloping for all he was worth.

Slow as Ollie was, he stretched for the bag and beat the throw, and the Scrappers finally had a hit—if it wasn't ruled an error.

Chad was coming up, and Thurlow couldn't picture him even putting the ball in play against Salinas. But Thurlow had an idea. "Coach," he said, and he walked out to the coach's box.

Coach Carlton yelled to the umpire, "Time-out."

"I was just thinking," Thurlow said. "Chad will never get his bat on the ball the way Salinas is throwing. But he bunts pretty well. If he could get the ball down, and if we could get Ollie to second, the top of the order is coming up. We might be able to get a run across."

"I was thinking about that. But Ollie's aw-fully slow. If it's not a great bunt, they might throw him out at second."

"Yeah. Maybe. But Chad's almost a sure strikeout if he swings away. The other way, we might have a shot."

Coach nodded. "All right. It's worth a try. Thanks."

"Sure," Thurlow said, and he walked back to the dugout. He liked the way he felt, and he appreciated the coach being willing to listen.

Chad got the bunt signal, but the first time he tried to lay the ball down, he popped it up. He was just lucky that it fell out of Flowers's reach, in foul territory.

Now the surprise was gone, and the infielders moved in closer. But the coach stayed with the bunt. Chad almost went after a high pitch but then pulled back in time to avoid a second strike.

Thurlow wondered. Maybe the coach would take the signal off now and try to cross up the defense. But that still didn't make sense to Thurlow. Chad just didn't swing the bat well enough.

Coach Carlton was apparently thinking the same thing. Chad squared off again, and this time he got the ball down. Stein was playing in at third, and he charged, but Ollie had broken hard for second. Stein had to go to first with the throw.

So there were two outs, but Ollie was in scoring position. And maybe Salinas had a little something to think about.

Jeremy was up, and he waited Salinas out. The big guy always seemed to struggle to get the ball into Jeremy's small strike zone. He ended up walking him for a second time.

Now Robbie and Gloria were coming up. If anyone could make something happen against Salinas, they were the ones who could do it.

Salinas's first pitch zapped past Robbie like a passing bullet, but it stayed high. And then Salinas tried a curve that broke a little wide.

This was one of the few times Salinas had been behind on a batter. Robbie knew his baseball. Thurlow was sure he would be looking for a fastball, maybe with a little less on it this time.

Sure enough, the next pitch didn't come with as much smoke, and Robbie was ready. He slammed a long fly into the left center gap, past Sheri Gibby. She did a great job of cutting the ball off before it rolled to the fence, but she had no chance to get Ollie at home. She threw toward third, and Jeremy had to hold up at second.

Thurlow's idea had worked, and now, if Gloria could come through, the Scrappers could get the game tied—or even break out on top.

The trouble was, Gloria just hadn't been herself at the plate lately. She seemed way too eager to make something happen. She reached for an outside pitch and dribbled a little roller toward Pingree. He picked it up and stepped on first, and the inning was over.

Still, the Scrappers had cut the lead in half, and now they knew they could scrap out a run against Salinas. If they could do it once, they could do it again. They just needed to keep the Mustangs from scoring any more.

Pingree was up first in the fourth inning, and the Mustangs were all yelling to him to get something going. They had to be a little uncomfortable, not to have broken out with more runs themselves.

Ollie was still focused, and he crossed up Pingree with a nice curve for a strike to start things out. But Pingree was clearly looking for a fastball on the next pitch, and he got it. He met the ball and drove a fly to right field.

He didn't get it all. It should have been caught, but Chad got a late start, and then he didn't have the speed to make up for it. The ball got past him, in the gap, and it was Jeremy who had to run it down and throw back to the infield.

Pingree trotted into second with a stand-up double.

Things looked better when Stabler hit another fly ball, this time to left, and Trent took care of it. But then Stein got hold of one. He drove a line drive between Chad and Jeremy. Jeremy flew to the ball, and he cut it off in time to get it back to the infield quickly. He held Stein to a single and kept Pingree from scoring, but now there were runners on first and third with only one out.

Thurlow could hardly breathe. He could see this game going down the drain, and there was nothing he could do about it. The Mustangs were trying to go to right field whenever they could. That was obvious. And why shouldn't they? That's where the Scrappers were weak.

Salinas got fooled by a curve, however, and he hit a ball almost straight in the air. Wilson camped under it and made the catch.

Maybe the Scrappers could dodge another bullet.

But Lou was up, and he was a battler. He took some pitches, fouled some off, and then the umpire called a ball on a 3 and 2 count. From where he was, Thurlow thought the pitch was a strike, but he had no angle. The simple fact was, the bases were loaded with Flowers coming up.

Ollie's face didn't change. He looked determined, even sure of himself. And he started well. He got ahead of Flowers with a called strike on the inside edge. But when he went outside with the next pitch, Flowers reached out and knocked a shot down the right field line. When it whizzed past Adam, Thurlow was sure the ball would roll to the corner and clear the bases.

Chad made a great effort, though. He took a good angle, got to the ball as fast as he could, and then he turned and threw to Tracy. Two runs had scored, but Tracy made the pivot and a good throw home. Lou was out by a mile.

The top of the inning was over, but the damage had been done.

The score was 4 to 1. The hill the Scrappers had been trying to climb now looked like a mountain.

As the players filed into the dugout, Thurlow heard them saying all the right things, but he could see in their eyes and hear in their voices that they were beginning to give up. And he couldn't blame them. With Chad out there, what could they do?

Thurlow saw that the coach was standing away from the dugout. He was talking to Thurlow's mom. Thurlow walked out to them, mostly just curious to find out what they were saying.

Coach looked at Thurlow. "We're wondering—should we have Jeremy cheat more toward right field and give Chad some help?"

"Trent's not all that fast either," Thurlow said. "I've always played a little to the left and tried to help him. But then, I always know that Jeremy can cover plenty of ground when he's in right."

"But, Thurlow, you're *not* out there," Wanda said. "So what can we do with the team that *is* on the field?"

"I don't know," Thurlow said. His mom sounded about half angry, and he couldn't figure that out. What was she accusing him of now?

"Well, now, that's not Thurlow's problem. That's mine," Coach Carlton said. "I'm going to have Jeremy play a little more toward right. It's a gamble, but it's the only thing we can do."

Thurlow walked back to the dugout. But he felt uneasy about the coach's decision. As he sat down on the dugout steps, he heard Chad say, "I'm sorry, everybody. I'm trying my best. . . . But how am I supposed to fill in for Thurlow?"

"Hey, that's no way to think," Thurlow said, but he knew he was talking to himself as much as he was to Chad. And now his brain was searching for answers. "Ollie," he said, "you've been throwing outside a lot, trying to keep those guys from pulling the ball, right?"

"Sure."

"But they're starting to go with the pitch, and they're hitting to the right side. That's putting more pressure on Chad."

Ollie nodded. "Yeah. Sure. But those guys can go deep. I don't want to pitch to their power."

"They won't hit the ball out of the park, Ollie. This field is too big. Why not come to the inside of the plate? And have Trent play deep?"

"The deeper he is, the wider the gaps," Coach Carlton said. He had walked up behind Thurlow. "If they hit line drives, we may not get to them."

"Maybe so. But what we're doing now isn't working. Isn't it worth a try?"

The coach didn't answer. He was thinking.

"I've got another idea," Chad said. "Put Cindy in right field. She's better than I am—faster and a better fielder. I know you usually put her in the infield, but she can play outfield just as well."

"Chad, don't be so hard on yourself," Coach Carlton said. "You've done all right."

"But we don't have the best team on the field," Chad said. "Cindy hits better than I do, too. If you put her in later for Tracy—the way you usually do—then we lose Tracy from the lineup, and she's another good hitter."

"Are you sure you would feel okay about that?"

"Sure. I want to win this game."

Thurlow couldn't believe it. He had never in his life thought that way. But he had to admire Chad.

"All right," Coach Carlton said. "When we go back out on the field, you go in for Chad, Cindy. And, Ollie, don't start thinking about spots so much that you aim the ball, but don't stay away from the batters all the time the way you've been trying to do. Waste a pitch outside once in a while, and then come back to the inside. They're all crowding the plate. Maybe you can bust them inside and they'll hit the ball off the handle. Or if they do power one, Trent can play deeper than usual."

"What we need right now are some runs!" Gloria yelled.

And the team picked up the chatter.

Coach Carlton turned to Thurlow. "Thanks," he said.

"It might backfire," Thurlow told him.

"I know. But I like what you're doing. You're trying to figure a way to help us win on a day when you can't play."

The coach walked away from the dugout. Wanda started to follow him, but Thurlow said, "Mom," and she looked back. "I do want to be on this team," he said.

"You just made a good start," she said, and she smiled. And then she stepped closer and whispered, "If you ran your hardest today—with your ankle hurt—do you think you could outrun Chad?"

"No."

"Well, now you know how he feels. He's doing the best he can with the talent he's got. It's good for you to sit over here and see it that way for a day."

"I wasn't putting him down, Mom."

"No. I understand that. I liked what you said. But just remember, a ballplayer has only so many God-given talents. The rest is attitude. A really great player has to have that, too."

Thurlow nodded. And when his mother walked away, he considered the kind of teammate he had been most of the season. He was surprised when the thought occurred to him, but he realized that in some ways, Chad was a better guy to have on the team than he was.

CHAPTER EIGHT

Wilson had never had a lot of success against Salinas. But today he was completely baffled. He took some good rips, but he struck out again.

Trent had a better idea, however. He waited for a good pitch and then took a compact swing and punched the ball into center for a single.

That was what the Scrappers needed: base runners. The players stood and cheered for Trent, and then they yelled to Tracy to keep it going.

She got off to a bad start when she watched a strike go by. But then Salinas threw wild, inside. Tracy spun out of the way, but the ball clipped her hip.

Tracy wasn't hurt. In fact, she seemed only too happy to get a free ride to first base—any way she could get it.

Now the Scrappers needed a big hit, or maybe another break.

But it didn't happen. Salinas bore down and struck out Adam, and then he got Ollie on a comeback grounder, right to the mound.

Thurlow slammed his fist against his leg. The fourth inning was over. There would only be three more chances. What else could the Scrappers do? How could they score some runs? He had to come up with something, not just sit there.

But it was one thing to make an adjustment in the outfield; it was something else to send batters to the plate to face the best pitcher in the league. Unless the Mustangs made some mistakes on defense, there really didn't seem to be much hope.

For now, the Scrappers had to get the side out. Thurlow hoped that Ollie wouldn't try to change what he had been doing and cross *himself* up. But he threw Mauer a fastball, well outside, and then came back with a burner in close. Mauer swung hard but hit the ball off the handle and popped it up. Gloria took the ball for out number one.

Donaldson was up next. Ollie was probably

trying to come inside with the first pitch, but he got it out over the plate. Thurlow cringed when he saw Donaldson get around on it and *launch* it to left field.

The Mustangs' fans let out an enormous roar. The ball sailed way back . . . *way* back . . . and right into Trent's glove! Thurlow's plan had worked.

Thurlow watched Ollie take a big breath, and then he went after Gibby with new confidence. He worked in and out, wasting outside pitches, going for outs on the inside. Gibby chased a couple of those outside tosses and then swung and missed on a pitch in on her fists. Strike three.

Now it was time to get those runs. Cindy was up. Maybe she could do what Chad hadn't done: get something going at the bottom of the order. But Salinas was too much for her, too. He seemed to be getting stronger as the game went on. She took some pitches, obviously hoping for a walk, but she finally struck out on a pitch that was in the catcher's glove before she got the bat around.

Jeremy had to be hoping for a walk, since he had gotten to first twice that way already. But

Salinas found the strike zone with his first pitch, and after missing high, he got another one in to make the count 1 and 2.

Jeremy didn't panic. He watched closely as Salinas let a couple pitches sail high again. Now Salinas had to throw a full-count strike. He did, but Jeremy was ready. He timed his swing and knocked a hard grounder past Stabler into left field.

"Okay, Robbie, this is it," Thurlow shouted. "This time you do it." The words had come out of Thurlow before he had expected them. He was not the kind of guy to yell and cheer, never had been, but there was nothing else he could do now.

Robbie stepped to the plate, took a couple of easy practice swings, and then got set. Just then Thurlow thought of something. "Coach, call a time-out," he said.

"Time!" Coach called, and he looked over at Thurlow. "What's going on?" he said.

"Call Robbie over here."

The coach waved Robbie back, and Thurlow walked out to meet with him and the coach. He had forgotten all about any pain in his foot now. "Robbie," he said, "everyone's been trying to wait Salinas out. He keeps gunning his first pitches over the plate. Once he gets a couple of strikes, he messes around some. So you might get your best shot on the first pitch."

Robbie looked at Coach Carlton. Gloria, who was on deck, had walked over and was listening, too.

"That might be right," he said to Thurlow. "But I don't like to tell a batter that." He looked back at Robbie. "If you go up there thinking that you'll swing at the first pitch, you might just swing at ball one."

"I know. But Thurlow's right. We've all been waiting and getting behind. I'm going to swing if the pitch is there."

"Well, sure. Salinas hasn't given up a lot of walks. We won't get anywhere hoping for that."

So Robbie walked back to the plate and got set again. And when the first pitch came down the middle, like a dagger, Robbie met it with a smooth, level swing.

The ball pinged off his bat and shot into center field. Thurlow jumped to his feet. He thought for sure the ball was hit long enough for extra bases.

But Donaldson was "on his horse," going

hard. He turned his back and ran straight away from the infield, and then, just when it seemed the ball would sail over his head, he spun around, reached up, and snagged it. He fell backward and had to jump up to throw back to his cutoff, but Jeremy had gone halfway to second, expecting the ball would drop, and now he had to go back to first.

Thurlow heard Tracy say, "These guys are *so* good." He expected someone to chew her out, to tell her that the Scrappers were better. But the team was sitting back down, after having jumped up following Robbie's bullet, and now most of them were staring at the floor, looking defeated.

Thurlow started to wonder if maybe there does come a time when you have to admit that you have met a better team, when you have to settle for second best. But what kind of an attitude was that? If he couldn't play, he had to figure out a way for his team to win this thing.

Gloria swung at the first pitch, too, but she missed. Then she got frustrated and swung at a bad pitch. "Gloria, don't be so stupid," she told herself, loud enough for everyone in the park to hear. Then she watched the next pitch pop into Flowers's glove, as though she were frozen in place.

"Steeee-rike three!" the umpire called.

Gloria didn't even argue. She was mad at herself, not at the umpire. As she walked back to the dugout, she cocked her arm, ready to throw her bat, but then she stopped herself. She looked at the players coming out of the dugout and said, "This game is *not* over. Do you hear me? We can get those runs. We just need to keep holding them until we can catch up."

No one said a word.

"Do you hear me? We can still win this game."

Finally, the players reacted. They shouted— a little—and they ran onto the field. Thurlow had no idea whether they believed what Gloria had said, but he had to hand it to them; they were still scrapping.

When Ollie went inside/outside once too often and didn't catch the plate, he walked Pingree. But the Scrappers told Ollie not to worry, and he came back with a great pitch on the inside edge to Stabler. Stabler cracked another long fly to left, but once again, Trent was in the right place. He made the catch, and Pingree had to go back to first.

Stein also got around on a pitch, but he knocked it to the left side on the ground. It darted into the hole between Robbie and Gloria. Both broke for it, but it was Robbie who cut in front, stretched out, and made the stab, and then, still running toward second, flipped the ball to Tracy.

Thurlow was glad that Robbie had gotten the lead runner. He didn't think there was a chance for two. But it didn't matter what *he* thought. Tracy dragged her left foot across the bag, then made the turn and shot the ball on a line to Adam.

It was a bang-bang play at first, but the umpire shouted, "Out!"

The crowd gave the Scrappers a huge ovation, and Thurlow knew that the only way that much noise could come out of the stands was if supporters for both teams were giving the players— maybe on both teams—credit for what they were seeing.

The Scrappers ran back to the dugout and sat down, but Thurlow wasn't hearing much out of them, couldn't see any hunger in their eyes. Suddenly he found himself walking along in front of them, looking into their faces. "Hey, those guys are good. But so are we. Do you believe that?"

"Yeah!" the players shouted

"All right. This is the inning. We need runs—now!"

Gloria was laughing. "Hey, look who's turned into a cheerleader," she said.

Thurlow laughed, too, but he told her, "I don't care. That's all I can be today. So you guys need to get it done out there."

"Hey, you're walking pretty well," Wilson said. He was standing by the bat rack, outside the dugout. "Maybe you better get your shoes on and do it yourself."

Thurlow wished he could. "I can't. But you guys can. Play it smart. Poke the ball. Put it in play. We need runners."

"All right!" Wilson said, and he walked toward the batter's box.

Thurlow walked over and sat down on the stairs. The Mustangs hadn't lost any of their fire either. The infield was talking it up, big-time. "Six more outs. That's all we need," Thurlow heard Pingree yelling to the other infielders.

That, of course, was true. And Thurlow also knew that the top of the order had had its shot in the fifth. If Salinas kept mowing people down, he could get out of the game without facing the heart of the batting order again.

Wilson tried hard to shorten his swing, but that only seemed to throw his timing off. The big guy looked destroyed when he swung at a curveball and struck out and then had to walk back to the dugout.

Thurlow heard the countdown in his head. Five outs to go.

But then Trent hit a stinger of a grounder past Pingree into right field, and Tracy surprised everyone with a drag bunt. It worked to perfection. Pingree charged the ball, but by the time he got to it, there was no hope to throw out Tracy at first.

Another chance. Another scrappy play.

But Adam bounced an easy grounder to Mauer. Mauer tossed to Stabler at second, who made a perfect relay to first. The Mustangs had their own double play, and now the crowd was cheering for them.

Just like that, the count was down to only

three outs left for the Scrappers.

Coach Carlton walked over to the dugout. "Martin," he called. "Come here."

"Coach," Thurlow said, "the Mustangs aren't substituting. They haven't made a single change."

"I know. But that's not how we play it. We all play—in every game. We can't leave Martin out of the biggest game of the season."

But Martin stepped out from the dugout and said, "It's all right, Coach. Don't put me in. I don't want to mess up."

"Nope. I was willing to put Cindy in the outfield instead of taking Tracy out. But I won't change my rule about everybody playing. Go out and play first for Adam."

"Coach, I don't want to. Not now."

"Go on in, son. And do your best."

Thurlow felt his nerves take another jolt. And yet, it did seem right. This was how the Scrappers had done it all season, and it wouldn't be right to leave Martin on the bench now.

"All right, let's go!" Thurlow yelled. "Everybody be alive out there." He shook his fists at the players. "Let's hear some noise."

Salinas was coming up. He could not only

pitch; he could hit. He slapped a fastball up the middle for a single. Lou hit a fly ball to Jeremy after that, but then Flowers bounced a grounder past first base for another single, and Salinas rounded second and cruised into third.

Thurlow had almost given up a dozen times in this game. Now he found himself fighting against the feeling that the game was about to get out of reach.

But Ollie came back strong and got ahead of Mauer 0 and 2. Then Mauer fought off an inside pitch and bounced it toward Gloria. The play would normally be to second, for the force, but she had to charge the ball, and there was no hope to get a double play.

What she saw was Salinas breaking for the plate, and she fired home. Salinas slid hard, but Wilson stayed tough and put the tag on him. The run was cut down, and the Scrappers hadn't fallen any further behind.

"Great play!" Thurlow shouted.

Ollie sucked in some air and stared at the plate. He fired the hardest pitch of the night. It popped into Wilson's glove like a balloon breaking. Donaldson backed out of the box, took a breath of his own, and got back in.

Ollie wasn't messing with any kind of finesse now. He fired another heater. Donaldson took a hard cut and knocked a ground ball up the middle. Gloria flashed to the ball, stopped herself as best she could, and made a hard, off-balance throw.

The ball was wide and into the runner. Martin was pulled off the bag, but he made the catch and then swung his glove at Donaldson. He caught him on the shoulder, and the umpire yelled, "Out!"

So one more time, the Scrappers had stopped these guys. And Martin had come through. But the score was still 4 to 1, and now there was only one more chance.

CHAPTER NINE

Bottom of the seventh. The whole season on the line. And Salinas still throwing explosives.

The Scrappers—somehow—had to get scrappier. They had to do something different, make something happen.

Ollie and Cindy were coming up first. Thurlow was afraid there would be two outs before the top of the order got a chance. If only the team had some pinch hitters who could get the job done—but everyone had played.

Robbie walked over to Thurlow. "Thurlow," he said, "do you know anything about the 1988 World Series, when the Dodgers beat the Oakland A's?"

Thurlow was a nervous wreck, and now Robbie wanted to talk about the '88 World Series. "I don't know," Thurlow said. "Can you think of anything we can do to—"

"In the first game—in the ninth inning, with two outs—when it looked like the Dodgers had lost the game, the manager sent Kirk Gibson up to bat. He had a sprained ankle—a bad one. But he hit a two-run homer, won the game, and then limped around the bases."

Now Thurlow was staring at Robbie. The Scrappers did have a guy who hadn't played. But . . .

"Robbie, the coach won't let me. My mom won't either."

"I know you can't do it until there are two outs. If you had to run hard, you wouldn't be able to do much and you could risk permanent damage. But with two outs, it would be all or nothing."

"It wouldn't mean a thing if we didn't have some runners on."

"I know. It's just a thought." Then he walked away.

Thurlow put his weight on his right foot, tried to feel whether he could get the kind of leverage he needed. His ankle did hurt when he did that, but . . . what if he wrapped it tighter?

Could he get his baseball shoe on over the wrap?"

No. It was stupid. Everyone would think he was showing off. He had to think of the team—and not always assume that he had to do everything.

Ollie was stepping into the box. Maybe he could get something started.

Salinas threw an arrow for a strike, but then he got a couple of pitches up, and Ollie got ahead 2 and 1. But the battle had only begun. Ollie swung and missed again, and then Salinas threw another ball, high. Full count.

Ollie kept fighting off the hard stuff, flicking foul balls down the first base line, and the count stayed full for three pitches. Then Salinas let one get away from him, way high.

Ollie walked.

"All right! We can do this!" Thurlow yelled. "Cindy, stay tough. Make him pitch to you."

But Salinas was mad at himself for walking Ollie. He threw three rockets over the plate. Cindy took the first two and then swung and missed on the third.

One away. Just two more chances. Thurlow

had to do something. What Robbie had said made sense—if he could get his shoe on. Thurlow stepped down off the dugout steps. He pointed to Robbie, then to Gloria. "You two have to keep this going—no matter what. Do you hear me?"

"I hear you," Robbie said. "Are you going to . . ."

Thurlow turned and walked into the tunnel behind the dugout, toward the college locker room.

Behind him, he heard Robbie say. "Hurry, Thurlow. We *will* keep it going."

Thurlow's shoes were in a locker, in his duffel bag. He grabbed the bag and sat down.

"Next batter, Jeremy Lim," the announcer was saying.

Thurlow pulled off his sandal, undid his ankle wrap, and then began to wrap it tighter. By then Jeremy had worked the count to 2 and 2. Maybe he could get another walk.

But just as Thurlow was putting the hooks in the stretch wrap to hold it in place, the announcer said, "Two away. Next batter, Robbie Marquez."

Maybe it was too late. Maybe Robbie would

strike out, too, and that would be the end of it. But Robbie had vowed.

Thurlow got his left shoe on and tied it, quickly. Then he pulled the laces on the right one as loose as he could, and he forced his foot into it. The pain was pretty bad when he shoved his heel in, and even worse when he pulled the laces tight.

Just as he was about to tie the lace, pain or not, he heard the crowd cheer, and he stopped. Maybe the game was over.

But when the noise calmed, the announcer said, "Next batter, Gloria Gibbs." Robbie had done it. Somehow. He had gotten on base.

Thurlow tied the lace as tight as he could stand it, and then he stood up and tested the ankle with all his weight on the right foot. It wasn't all that bad. He hurried back out to the dugout. Just as he got there, he saw Gloria swing and miss.

She had had nothing but trouble with Salinas all night. But Thurlow knew that she was the toughest player on the team when the game was on the line. If there was a way to get on, she would find it.

Thurlow looked around the field. Ollie was

at second, Robbie at first. So the force was on at all three bases. With two outs, the Mustangs could play back and take the easy one. Everything was against Gloria.

But she was standing outside the box, and she was psyching herself up. She picked up some dirt, rubbed it on her hands, and then wiped a streak across her shirt. When she stepped back in, she looked ready to kill.

But that's not what she did. She got a curveball, and she didn't get antsy. She waited on it and then took an easy swing. She looped the ball to right field.

Mauer ran hard, but he couldn't reach it. The ball dropped in!

Lou charged the ball and made a strong throw. Ollie had to stop at third.

Bases loaded. Two out. Tying run on base. The crowd was going nuts. Now was the time.

Wilson was walking to the plate, but Thurlow hurried out of the dugout and straight to the coach. "Just a sec," Thurlow said.

The coach called a time-out, then looked at Thurlow.

"I was just thinking that you might want me to pinch-hit for Wilson," he said.

"What?"

"Come here," Thurlow yelled to Wilson. Then he said to Coach Carlton, "I got my shoe on. It feels okay. I can put weight on my foot well enough to swing all right."

"But you can't run, can you?"

"Not the way I usually can." Then he grinned. "But I can probably run as fast as Wilson."

"No, Thurlow. I told you. I can't let you take a chance on hurting that ankle again."

"It's just one play. I'll be all right."

But the coach was still shaking his head.

"Coach, I'm not trying to show off. I just think this is our best shot." He glanced at Wilson, who was walking up to them. "Wilson has struck out every time. Salinas is really tough on him. I have the quickest bat on the team. I have a better chance of getting around on the ball than anyone. I'm not bragging. I just know I'm right."

"He'll throw away from you, not let you pull the ball."

"I'll hit it to right if he does that. If I can't hit it out, I'll run to first and stop. I'll just try to keep the game going—keep the team alive."

The umpire was shouting now, telling the coach it was time to do something. But Wanda was trotting across the field. "He can't play, if that's what you're thinking," she was saying as she approached.

"He's going to bat," Coach Carlton said. "He's promised me he'll be careful about running."

"But he—"

"Wanda, I think this is the way to go. What Thurlow said makes sense. Let's use every weapon we've got. If he hits a ground ball, he won't be able to run hard. But if he can hit one in a gap and run as far as first, we still have something going. I can pull him back out—because of the injury—and put in a runner."

Wanda put her hand on Thurlow's shoulder. "I don't like this," she said. "It scares me."

"It's okay, Mom. Trust me, for once."

"All right. I will," she said. "But if you try to be a hero and twist that ankle—"

"I won't do that."

"Let's have a batter," the ump was shouting.

"All right," the coach hollered back to him. And then he looked at Wilson. "How do you feel about this?"

Wilson was grinning. "Great!" he said. He looked relieved.

"Okay, ump. Coates is batting for Love."

Thurlow strode to the box. He tried not to limp, but his shoe was tight, and he couldn't walk quite as smoothly as he wanted to.

"Now batting, Thurlow Coates," the announcer said. The crowd responded, made a noise like a jet engine warming up. This was the great moment of the season—for both teams.

Salinas nodded at Thurlow, even smiled a little, and Thurlow smiled back. "Come on, Salinas," he whispered to himself. "Let's see what you've got." He planted his weight on that right foot and felt some pain, but it wasn't too bad.

The first pitch was a big surprise. Salinas spun a curve that broke outside. Thurlow was looking for a fastball all the way. He started his swing, tried to hold up, but couldn't.

The awkward swing threw him off balance, and his ankle gave way. Thurlow dropped to his knees.

A big noise, like a collective sigh, came out of the crowd.

Thurlow scrambled up, and he tested the ankle again. It wasn't any worse. He got back in the box and waited. Salinas threw a fastball, outside, for a ball.

Then another one.

Thurlow could see what Salinas was going to do. He would rather walk in a run than give Thurlow something good to hit.

Thurlow moved closer to the plate. The next pitch was outside, too, but Thurlow reached for it. He hit it square, but he smashed a long foul down the right field line.

The count was 2 and 2.

Thurlow was down to one strike. He stepped out of the box. He looked at Salinas. Then he smiled and shook his head. He wasn't going to say anything, but he was trying to say to the guy, "You don't dare pitch to me, do you?"

He saw Salinas nod, and now he thought he might get his chance.

He stepped to the plate and got set again. The ball was a thunderbolt, a high fastball, over the plate.

Thurlow didn't think about his ankle, didn't think about anything but that white ball.

He saw it clearly, and he reacted.

The bat seemed to leap to the ball, as if by it-self. He felt no pain, no awkwardness. He felt only the bat as it connected—rock solid.

Thurlow had never hit a ball so hard.

It sailed long and high . . . rising, rising. It was hit to the deepest part of the field, just left of center, but there was no doubt where it would land. The outfielders weren't running; they were looking up. And the ball seemed to travel forever—out into the night.

Grand slam! The Scrappers had won the championship.

But Thurlow had hardly realized that yet. There was something pure—perfect—about hitting a baseball that well, that far. And the quiet in the park was pure, too.

The ball disappeared into the dark, and then a roar finally broke the silence. Thurlow began to trot, but now the pain was there. He tried not to limp, but he couldn't help it. He favored his bad foot all the way around the bases.

In spite of the pain, he didn't want to reach the end of this run, to get to home plate. He wanted to feel this way forever. But as he rounded third, he knew there was something better than being out on the field alone. He wanted to be with his teammates, and they were waiting at home plate. They probably weren't the best players in the league, but they were the scrappiest, and they had won it all.

As he limped toward the plate, he could see that they knew better than to mob him. Instead, they just collected around him. They were surprisingly quiet, as though they were still in shock, not quite sure that this had really happened.

Someone tried to pick Thurlow up, to carry him off, but he wouldn't let that happen. He found the coach instead and shook his hand. "Thanks," he said. "Thanks for everything. Thanks for letting me bat."

The coach pulled him close and hugged him. "You're going to play in the big leagues someday, Thurlow," he said. "You're the best young player I've ever seen."

Then Wanda was there, pulling Thurlow to her. "I'm so proud of you," she told him.

It was all a little more than Thurlow knew how to handle.

By then the announcer was calling for the teams to take the field to receive their trophies.

But every player wanted to slap Thurlow on the back or thank him for coming through. And he wanted to tell all of them how great they had played. He talked to every one of them individually.

But gradually the Scrappers arranged themselves in a line on the left side of the mound, and the Mustangs gathered on the other side. Thurlow looked over at Salinas, who was looking back at him. Salinas nodded, and the motion said, "Congratulations. You got me." He looked pretty unhappy, but there was a lot of respect in his eyes.

The league officials came down the line and gave a little trophy to each of the Mustangs and then a larger one to each of the Scrappers. Finally, they gave a big glass trophy to Mr. Gibbs, the Scrappers' sponsor. He held it high in the air and laughed like a foghorn. At last the Scrappers let loose, sent up a cheer for themselves.

When the ceremony ended, the parents collected around, and the coach gave one last speech. "These trophies are awfully nice," he said. "But you might lose them or break them or stick them in the back of some closet. What no one here will lose is what you've learned. You became a team this summer—a real team—and every single one of you did what it took to be a champion."

Thurlow looked up and down the line at the players. It was amazing to think how far they had come—and how much he liked every one of them: Jeremy, Robbie, Gloria, Wilson, Trent, Tracy, Adam, Ollie, Cindy, Chad, Martin. The coach. And his mom. He was glad she had made him play.

Thurlow knew that life was pretty long and that he had a lot of great things to look forward to, but he suspected that he wouldn't experience many moments that would be quite as fine as this one. No matter how old he got, he would remember that ball, that white speck, disappearing into the night sky.

Grand slam!

The championship!

TIPS FOR PLAYING RIGHT FIELD

1. Some kids get the idea that right field is the quiet spot on the field. But that isn't true. If your team has a good pitcher, many right-handed batters will swing late. Right field can often be "where the action is."

2. No one on the team needs a stronger arm than the right fielder. A right fielder often has to throw all the way to third—one of the longest, hardest throws in baseball.

3. Study batters. Get to know them. Don't shift right just because a right-handed batter comes up. Some batters pull the ball, but others have a hard time getting around on a fast pitcher. So think about who's pitching, too.

4. Catch as many fly balls as you can in practice—and then go home and catch some more. It's a skill you can learn only through lots of hard work. One time you may be catching a looping fly in front of you, and the next time a long shot over your head. The only way to learn all the different kinds of catches is to make them all—lots of times.

5. Outfielders actually handle more ground balls than fly balls, so don't forget about your fielding. Along with all those flies you're catching, have someone hit grounders to you, too.

6. When a ground ball is hit your way, run hard to get in front of it. Then, if you have time, go down on one knee as you field it. That way, if the ball gets past your glove, you'll block it and it won't get through your legs.

7. Learn to work with your center fielder. Call for a ball that is clearly yours—but when in doubt, the center fielder makes the decision. If the center fielder calls for the ball, don't stop where you are. Cut behind the center fielder and become a backup.

8. Don't try to be a hot dog. Catch the ball with both hands whenever you can, and catch it up where you can watch the ball all the way into your glove.

9. When you throw the ball to the infield, don't toss a rainbow. Gun the ball low and hard, on a line. It's better for the ball to bounce in front of the infielder than to float slowly through the air.

10. The cutoff for the right fielder is often the second baseman. Don't "come up throwing" and just toss the ball to a base. Look for the *player* you're throwing to, and get the ball in as quickly as you can. A lazy outfielder will often allow a runner to take an extra base.

SOME RULES FROM COACH CARLTON

HITTING:

Take a stance that is comfortable and natural. Some kids try to imitate a favorite major league player, but your natural stance may be very different from his. Hold the bat with your hands above your waist but not above your shoulders, and make sure you feel balanced and relaxed.

BASE RUNNING:

When on base, *think*. Know the outfielders you're playing against and how strong their arms are. How important is the run you carry? Is it a time to gamble or a time to play it safe? Is a double play a danger? Those things, and many others, should be going through your mind. So think what you're doing, listen to your coach, and forget about blowing kisses to your fans.

BEING A TEAM PLAYER:

When a game is over, shake hands with the opposing players. Give them credit if they won, and never put them down if they lost. The next game could be different!